The subject
vocabulary
with expert
brief and simple text is printed
in large, clear type.

Children's questions are
anticipated and facts presented
in a logical sequence. Where
possible, the books show
what happened in the past
and what is relevant today.

Special artwork has been
commissioned to set a standard
rarely seen in books for this
reading age and at this price.

Full-colour illustrations are on
all 48 pages to give maximum
impact and provide the
extra enrichment that is the
aim of all Ladybird Leaders.

A Ladybird Leader

# the tree
## and its world

written by Romola Showell

illustrated by Sean Milne and Frank Humphris

Publishers: Ladybird Books Ltd . Loughborough
© Ladybird Books Ltd 1975
*Printed in England*

This is a tree.

It is an oak tree.

You know that it is old because the
trunk is so big and the bark is so thick

Young oak trees have smooth bark,
grey in colour.
But as the tree gets older
the bark gets rough and ridged.

Oak wood is hard and strong,
and has been used
for furniture making,
ship building and
house building for
hundreds of years.

Oak trees live for a very long time.
They produce the best timber
when they are over
one hundred and fifty years old.

7

The buds of an oak tree look like this.

In the spring the buds open
and the leaves begin to grow.

The leaves look like this.

The seed of an oak tree
is called an acorn.

An oak tree does not have acorns until
it is more than sixty years old.

Each acorn has its own cup,
and years ago acorns were gathered
every Autumn for feeding the pigs
in the winter.

If an acorn falls on the soil
it will begin to grow.
A young oak tree grows from the acorn.
It needs water and soil to grow properly.

The oak tree has thick bark
and branches that spread out.

The branches are not too close together
and light can get through
between the leaves.

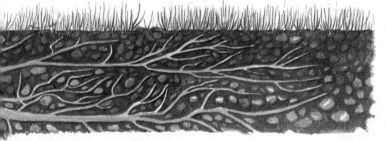

Under the ground
the roots spread out, too.

They spread as far under the ground
as the branches above the ground.

Some of the roots go deep into
the ground as well.

13

In the summer the branches
are covered with leaves,
and the ground under the tree
is shaded from sun and rain.

In autumn the leaves begin to fal

Trees that lose their leaves
in winter are called DECIDUOUS.

When all the leaves have gone
you can see the pattern
of the branches.

The green powdery growth seen on the bark of trees is really a very simple plant called an alga.

It grows best on the side that gets wet in the rain.

On some trees you can see
fungus growing.

Some fungi grow on living trees.

A fungus is a plant
but it has no green leaves.

This is a bracket fungus.

Mistletoe sometimes grows
on oak trees.

Mistletoe is a strange plant.

It will grow only on the branches of a
living tree.

The white mistletoe berries
contain the sticky seed.

Birds take the berries
and the seeds stick to their beaks.

The seeds will grow where they are
rubbed off on the rough bark.

19

Many birds will visit the oak tree
during a year.

If it is an old tree with holes in it
the little owl may nest
in one of the holes.

The little owl feeds on insects, mice,
small birds and, sometimes, frogs.

It hunts mainly at dawn and dusk
but it can be seen flying in the day time.

Owls swallow their food almost whole,
and then they spit out the parts
they cannot digest.

Owl 'pellets' made of fur,
insect cases and bones
can be found under
trees where owls
perch.

*Wood pigeon*

*Jackdaw*

Thrushes, jackdaws and blackbirds
are common visitors to any tree,
and the gentle 'coo coo' of the
wood pigeon is often heard from the
branches of the oak tree.

*Thrush*

*Blackbird*

Sometimes a tiny, brown bird
can be seen creeping up the trunk.

This is the tree creeper, and it is
hunting for insects in the bark.

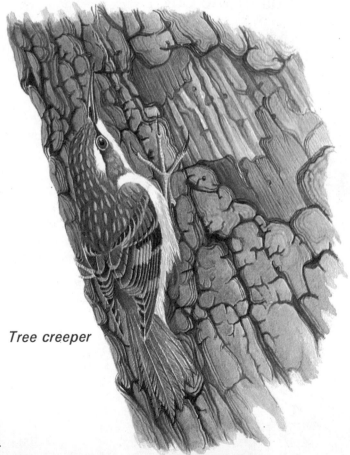

*Tree creeper*

*Great spotted woodpecker*

Another bird looking for grubs in the bark is the great spotted woodpecker. Its favourite food is the larvae (grubs) of beetles.

Some caterpillars feed on the leaves. The eggs are laid on the leaves by the moth or butterfly, and the caterpillars hatch out from the eggs.

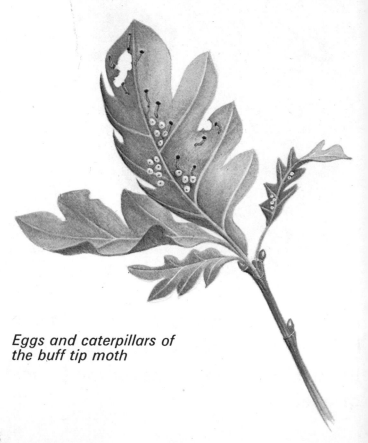

*Eggs and caterpillars of the buff tip moth*

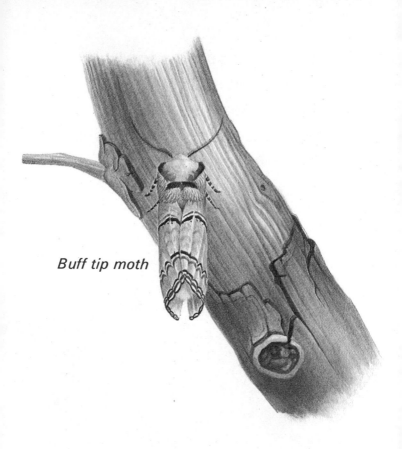

*Buff tip moth*

A very common moth is the buff tip.
It is found on the trees in woods.
When it rests on a twig it looks
like a piece of loose bark.

The buff tip lays its eggs
under the leaves,
and when they hatch
the yellow and black caterpillars
stay together in groups.
They eat the leaves.

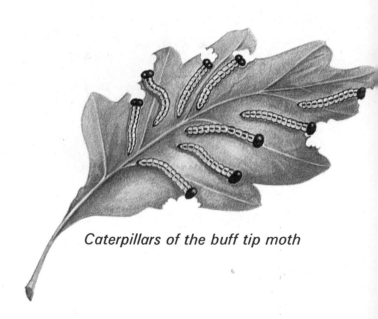

*Caterpillars of the buff tip moth*

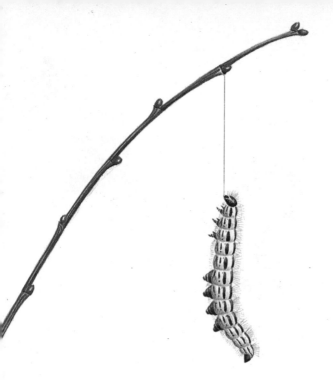

If the caterpillars are disturbed
they hang off the leaves
on silk threads
and lower themselves to the ground.

When the caterpillars are ready to
change into pupae
they bury themselves
in the soil round the tree.

*'Looper' caterpillar
of the mottled umber moth*

A moth starts as an egg,
hatches into a caterpillar,
and then changes into a pupa.
From this the adult moth will hatch.

Opposite is the caterpillar of the mottled umber moth (shown below).

It feeds on oak leaves.

It is called a 'looper' caterpillar because of the way it walks.

*Mottled umber moth*

Bark beetles make tunnels
under the bark of trees.

The eggs are laid under the bark.

When the grubs hatch out
they eat out new tunnels.

The tunnels make patterns
in the bark.

The beetles and the grubs
gnaw out these tunnels
under the bark of many trees.

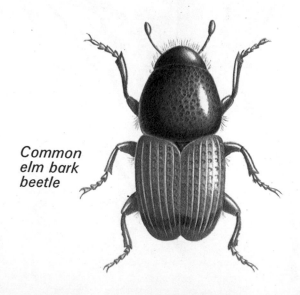

*Common
elm bark
beetle*

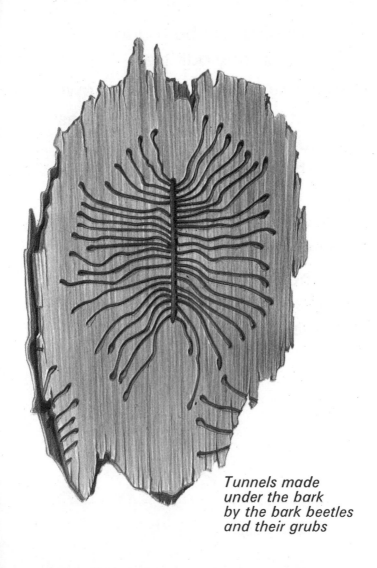

*Tunnels made under the bark by the bark beetles and their grubs*

33

Oak-apples can be found
on almost any oak tree.

They are round and pale brown.

Sometimes you find neat holes
bored in them
like those shown opposite.

Each oak-apple
contains the white larva of a wasp
called the gall wasp.

The hole shows
where the young adult wasp
chewed its way out.

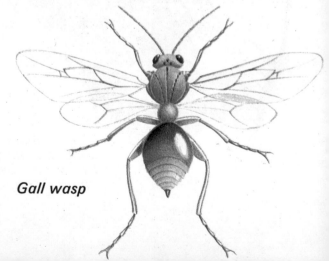

*Gall wasp*

*hole*

*Oak apples*

Spiders often live
on the rough bark of the tree.

They can hide in the cracks,
and come out from these
to hunt for their food.

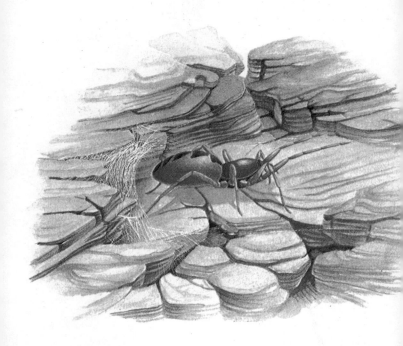

Their eggs are laid
in cocoons hidden under the bark.

Cocoons are spun by the spider
from spider-silk.

Tiny spiders
hatch from these eggs.

The grey squirrel runs up the trunk
of the tree so quickly that
it is often difficult to see.

Squirrels will eat acorns,
held between their front feet.

The squirrel can jump easily from
branch to branch.

It will often leap from one tree
to another.

They are less active
in winter but can
still be seen hunting for food
in the coldest weather.

The buried acorns
that the squirrel forgets
often grow into new trees.

An adult squirrel may eat
1½ lb. (680 gm)
of acorns in a week.

Other animals may visit the tree
from time to time.

The vole is a small animal
found in fields and woods.

It will nibble acorns and other seeds.

The vole is a pest because it eats
the bark of young trees.

It will also nibble off
the young shoots
of newly planted trees.

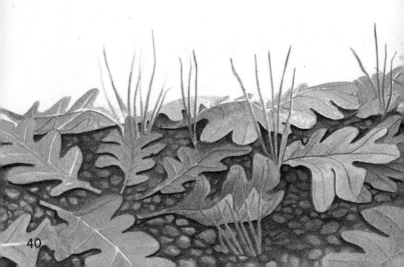

The long eared bat is found flying
among the branches of trees
hunting for food.

The bat sleeps during the daylight
and hunts at night.

Rabbits burrow
at the edge of woods,
and their holes
can be seen everywhere.

On sunny days the baby rabbits
will play under the oak trees
that grow in fields.

Under the tree,
where the fallen leaves collect,
you can find other small animals.

The fallen leaves are called 'litter'.

The animals that live in these leaves
don't like the light.

You will have to turn over the leaves
to find them.

The woodlouse
is a strange little animal.

One type – the pill woodlouse –
curls itself into a ball
when it is touched.

*Pill woodlice*

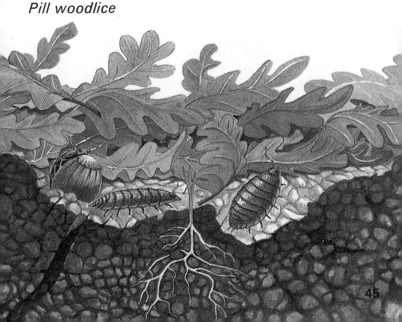

Earwigs and centipedes can be found under these damp leaves.

Although few people realise it, earwigs can fly well.

They have large wings tucked under the small wing cases.

The female earwig guards her eggs and looks after the baby earwigs.

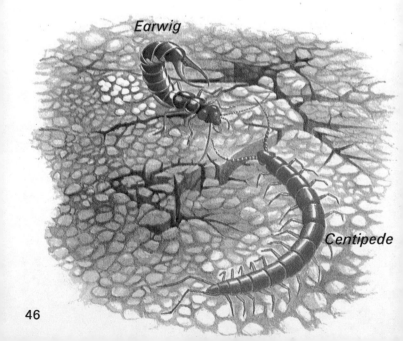

Earwig

Centipede

A very striking beetle
that is sometimes seen
is the stag beetle.

The larvae of these beetles
live mainly in the decaying branches
of old oak trees.

They also feed on dead root wood.

The tree needs water,
minerals from the soil
and sunlight, to make its food.

In turn it feeds the caterpillars
that live on its leaves,
and the squirrels
which eat its acorns.

The birds need the tree for roosting
and for nesting.

They eat the insects
that live on the tree.

A tree is a whole busy world.
Many small animals live on it,
and during its long life
many hundreds of them
will be protected by its branches.

This has been the story of one tree—
an oak tree.

Other trees are worth looking at, too.

Why don't you find out about
the other trees that you know?